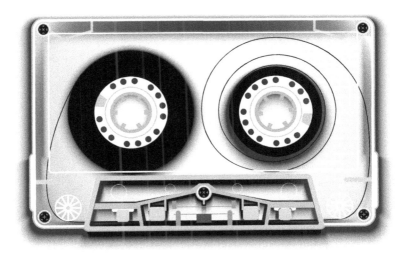

## *Also by John Osborne*

*Radio Head: Up and Down the Dial of British Radio* (Simon & Schuster, 2009)

*The Newsagent's Window* (Simon & Schuster, 2010)

*What if Men Burst in Wearing Balaclavas?* (Nasty Little Press, 2010)

*The New Blur Album* (Nasty Little Press, 2011)

*Most People Aren't That Happy, Anyway* (Nasty Little Press, 2013)

*Don't Need the Sunshine* (Automobile Association, 2013)

*No-one cares About Your New Thing* (Go Faster Stripe, 2017)

*A Supermarket Love Story* (Go Faster Stripe, 2021)

# *MY CAR PLAYS TAPES*

*Osborne*

ISBN: 978-1-915079-09-1

Cover design by Aaron Kent

Edited & Typeset by Aaron Kent

Broken Sleep Books (2022)

Broken Sleep Books Ltd
Rhydwen,
Talgarreg,
SA44 4HB
Wales

# *Contents*

# My Car Plays Tapes

John Osborne

We were in a pub. A big group of us at a table, crisps, real ale, telling jokes, and 'should we get more crisps?'

Absolutely.

He was friendly, the bloke I had a wee next to at the urinal, wearing an Idles t-shirt. 'Good pub this,' we both agreed, but back at the big table after a couple more beers and exchanging life updates we started talking about the news and we all admitted we were starting to get a bit scared now. How bad was this going to get? I can't remember it being like this, ever. It was hard to understand what was going on in the news, even though I listen to *The New Statesman* podcast which is really good, but when every episode finishes I think, yeah I haven't retained any of that.

Even though the world felt so horrible I was actually feeling pretty good about things. I'd started seeing someone new, which doesn't happen often, and I was worried it wouldn't work out, but let's see how it goes. That's what I say about everything now, let's see how it goes.

Sometimes I look at my friends and think yeah, we are all getting really old now. That's what I used to worry about more than anything but now that it's happening, I don't really mind it so much. Look at them; my adorable chubby middle-aged friends. I've slept on all their settees. Oh getting older, it's really hard. I guess my sister doesn't realise how rapidly her baby grows ... but I see it, in her WhatsApp photos. He is so beautiful in so many different ways, my tiny nephew, who has the same name as my boss and it's been much easier at work since I've been talking to them in the same way. 'You're tired. That's why you're so grumpy. Would you like some

banana? Don't get any on your tummy. Have you been up crying all night again? Your poor parents.'

One morning I was driving to work. On my last few journeys I'd thought this car doesn't feel right, I should definitely get it checked out at some stage, but I never quite got round to it. All the warning lights came on and I completely lost all power and the car completely stopped. Cars had to indicate and go round me. Hazards on, bonnet up, I just sat in the car completely distraught. I didn't know what to do. You know that feeling when something is entirely your responsibility and you don't know what to do. I just sat there, scared, confused. I don't know much about cars but I definitely felt this was bad. After about ten minutes another car pulled up behind me. This man got out and asked if I was okay?

I said … no. Not really.

He said I don't know much about cars … which wasn't exactly what I wanted him to say … but he helped me push it to the side of the road so it was out of the way and he waited with me while I phoned the RAC. He said the same thing had happened to him, a few months ago he'd been driving across Scotland and his car broke down. He had no mobile phone, it was the middle of the night, he didn't have a clue what to do, but someone stopped for him, and helped make sure he was okay. He said it's scary, isn't it.

When the RAC man arrived he went through my options, but said look, I've been a mechanic for 35 years, your car won't survive this. He looked at the mileage and said 'you've done well. Most cars don't get as many miles as you've done. Later that afternoon the car was scrapped; my beautiful Fiesta, that had never even had a puncture before. I was devastated, but something within me that day was revived, because of this complete stranger, who'd seen someone had a problem and checked that I was ok and he was in no rush to drive away.

I drive a lot with my job. I'm a support worker for adults with learning disabilities. I go from house to house, helping people who need help with their medication and cooking and getting out into the community. It's a good job. It's minimum wage but I like it. I write things too. Half my life as a support worker, the other half writing. I'm always in my car or at my desk.

One of my favourite people to support is someone who is non-verbal. She lives in a supported living house with three loud men with quite severe learning disabilities and she hates it there. It's too loud for her, there are always staff having conversations, coming and going, there's too much noise. On my first day I was told she really likes going out in the car. They said you won't believe the difference, she's so anxious and tense at home, but as soon as she's out in the car she's a completely different person. They said if you're ever on shift and want to take her out, she'd love that. So that's what we do. Whenever the house gets too loud I go and fetch my car keys. There's a café we've found that we both really like. It serves good coffee for £1.30, just off the A140, and she sits there with her decaf latte.

The café always plays the same music. Instrumental versions of soul songs. It feels right that there's no lyrics, just piano. We always sit at the same table, being served by the same waitress, ordering the same drinks, going in at the same time, and I loved sitting there, both of us listening to the music. The best songs aren't complicated you can play the melody with one finger. The people I like best aren't complicated either. They reply to your texts.

The first time we went to the café I thought this would be a good opportunity to get a book out or do some writing but I realised that would be rude. It took me a while to embrace this solitude, to realise she was given me permission to zone out of life, to get away from all the noise.

After I'd taken her out a few times I overheard two people I work with talking about her, and one of them said ... she seems to really like John. They seemed surprised. I'm not one to retweet my own reviews, but that felt a special thing to hear. I was so bad at my job when I started. I never knew what I should be doing and I was getting things wrong all the time.

But I was just starting to get the hang of it, and it was her I thought of when I sat in my broken-down Fiesta, waiting for the RAC to arrive. I don't have much going for me but at least I could offer her this continuity. How was I going to do my job if I didn't have my car?

I don't have much money. None of us do, support workers. Even the worst cars I saw for sale were beyond anything I could afford, but I knew someone who knew someone who knew someone who was getting rid of a Polo. I got their number and I gave them a call. She's called Georgina, she invited me around to have a look and she said I'm not going to ask for any money. This car has been with me my entire adult life. I just want to see it go to a good home. She said it's in good condition; her girlfriend is a mechanic, so it's been well looked after, but she said it's *really* old. She showed me the funny way the petrol cap opens and said it doesn't have electric windows so you have to wind them down, but that's good exercise for your elbows, and there's no CD player and the radio doesn't work. I don't suppose people really have tapes anymore, do they, but there's some Jamiroqui in the glove compartment I'll let you have that as well.

I said I might not know much about cars … but I've got tapes. If I had to describe myself in one sentence it would be someone who has kept their old cassette collection from the 1990s.

*Nightswimming* by REM was the first track on the first compilation tape my first proper girlfriend ever made for me.

I think about her every time I hear that song, which isn't often because I'm not really bothered about REM, but occasionally you'll hear it on TV, or in a pub, or it's played on Absolute Radio 90s.

A few weeks after getting that car, the Polo that plays tapes, I went to visit my dad. I went to my teenage bedroom and found all those old cassettes. Blur taped off Radio 1 in 1997 when they were performing live at Glastonbury. Songs taped off Mark Radcliffe's show and from the Top 40. I always had blank tapes ready so I could press play and record whenever a good song came on. I spent hours and hours working on these tapes. I think that's the happiest I've ever been, being a teenager, making these tapes. I liked being a teenager. I loved the melancholy and thinking about what life would be like one day.

And then I found it. A tape that says **For John** in *her* handwriting and as soon as I had her tape in my hand I immediately remembered every track in the right order. The Pixies, The Cranberries, Natalie Imbruglia.

I went downstairs. My dad had made me my tea. He's proud of his cooking these days. We talked about the weather,

Mourinho and the new Aldi near his house. We hugged goodbye, I took the tapes out to my car, put them in the glove compartment and as I headed out of the cul-de-sac I put in the *For John* tape.

I don't know what to do with nostalgia. I felt so disconnected from the person that *For John* tape had been made for. Those songs had been so important to me when I used to listen to that tape. If there was a fire it's that box of tapes I'd have saved, but now they're just a nostalgic curiosity. Listening to that tape it's like the words and instruments aren't there anymore, just the sound of faraway piano.

It was strange to think about that girl who had made me the *For John* tape. I've still got her brother's copy of *The Commitments* by Roddy Doyle and I thought about her dad when I heard Clive James had died. It's strange how we associate people in our heads. Someone told me she lives in New Zealand now, which feels like a lie, but I guess sometimes people do move to New Zealand. She'd never even been on a plane back when I knew her. I bet she's been on loads now. She was there when I passed my driving test and we all went out for a meal the day that she passed hers. Her mum had lasagne and her dad had half a rotisserie chicken. I don't know why I remember that.

It took a long time to feel right in this new car. The car that plays tapes. I missed my old Fiesta. I couldn't get used to the driving seat. This still felt like it was Georgina's car. Sometimes you don't feel right sitting in someone else's chair.

Another reason I drive a lot is because I do rural touring. Pretty much every support worker I work with has another job. Someone who started the same day as me does night shifts at a cider factory. There's a man who is also a window cleaner, and judging by his skills as a support worker ... probably not a very good one. A woman who has worked there for twenty-one years also runs a fruit and veg shop in Ipswich with her brother. For me, its rural touring. A few years ago I wrote a theatre show that has been popular with the type of people who book rural touring shows in village halls. So that's what I do. I get in my car and drive to village halls to do my show.

This is how these village hall shows always go:

They're always run by someone with a name like John Bailey or Avril. Sometimes you tell you they can stay at their house, sometimes you book yourself a Travelodge on an A-road or sometimes you just drive all the way back, overnight. Sometimes you're really looking forward to it, it's sunny and you arrive early and you have a pint in a nice pub in the afternoon ... but sometimes you think 'why am I doing this? Why have I driven 200 miles to do an old show in a village hall? What even is doing a gig in a village hall? I don't want to be doing this, I want to be in my flat. I don't spend any time there. I'm always in my car, working or in my car, driving to village halls.'

But ... John Bailey's a nice man. He makes you a cup of tea and tells you he's heard you on Radio 4, and that's always a nice thing to be told and you help unstack chairs to get the village hall ready for the show later that evening.

Before the show, you go back to where you're staying. You're shown up to where you'll be sleeping. This was their daughter's room. This is where she grew up. You can see the remains of blutack from where the East Seventeen and Keanu Reeves posters used to be. On the wall there's a photograph of their daughter smiling proudly on her graduation day. Next to her are her beaming mum and dad, John Bailey and Avril and you think those parents are downstairs waiting for me, we're about to go to the village hall and unstack chairs.

They tell me their daughter works for the British Embassy in Hong Kong and has two little girls, Esmé and Jenna

There's a bit of time before we need to head off so they leave you alone to freshen up. They show you the cord to pull to work the shower and they tell you performers in the village hall always stay in this room. Dara O'Brien stayed here once, before he was famous, a very nice man, they assure me, and I bet that when Dara O'Brien arrived in this room he will have put his bag on the bed and thought where am I?

I get my things together and go downstairs and say that I'm ready. Avril gets her torch out, John Bailey says goodbye to the dog and we set off to the village hall.

It's because I had no other options that I became a support worker. My writing work started to dry up. The rejection emails were becoming more frequent, but that's just what happens, isn't it. I'm surprised I'd made it last for so long. I'm proud of the things I have made. I've made theatre shows and have had books on the shelves in Waterstones. I've done so much more than I'd ever imagined. I've had my turn.

My friend Katie is a support worker. She's an artist too. She spends half her time painting, the other half being a support worker, and I like it when she tells me stories about the people she supports. One day she said to me I think you'd be good at that, so I decided to try … and now I'm a support worker too.

When the village hall show finishes, it's always the same. The first person to talk to you is always a man in with a worryingly red face and bright purple trousers who tells you he didn't know what to expect and hadn't planned to come along but he's friends with Avril, from church, and she's been telling him he needs to become more involved in community activities, and he actually thought it was quite good and how do I remember all of the words?

'So what do you do when you're not doing this?' people like him always ask me and it always makes me feel a bit awkward. I look around the village hall and say well '*this*' is sort of my life, really. '*This*' is what I do.

Sometimes when I'm talking to my successful friends about my career it's like I'm telling them about my Tamagotchi. Oh really? You're still keeping that alive.

Yeah... I am. I just like having something to hold in my pocket.

For a long time I didn't tell anyone I was a support worker. I didn't tell my friends or my dad or my sister. It feels strange, looking back now, but I didn't want people to know what

I was doing. Just after I'd started working there I went out drinking in London with my friend who is an actor. Her phone beeped, she looked at the text and said 'that was from Natalie Imbruglia.'

I guess that's what I was clinging on to. But what are we supposed to do with all of our achievements? Keep them in a big cardboard box at your dad's house that you have a look occasionally when you go back to visit at Christmas and think I really should go through that properly one day. So often when we're confronted with nostalgia it's for sad reasons, and that's why I was glad that I had this opportunity to listen to my old tapes.

Avril pays you a cheque and the village hall have given you the leftover wine and back home John Bailey says hello to the dog, Avril gets the cheese out and you sit at the big table and they tell you stories about their grandchildren. Avril says goodnight, loads the dishwasher and goes to bed with a book, and me and John Bailey stay up for another 25 minutes, drinking wine and talking about roads.

Then I go up to the bedroom where that teenage girl grew up, not realising that one day she'd work for the British Embassy in Hong Kong and she'd have two little daughters called Esmé and Jenna and that while she was living abroad her bedroom would become the spare room, where people like me and Dara O'Brien and probably John Hegley will all have stayed.

In the morning we'll get up early, me, Dara and John Hegley and we'll smell coffee being made downstairs. We'll go into the kitchen where Avril gives us a rack of toast and tells us that she made the jam herself, using gooseberries from the garden and now that it's daylight we'll see how beautiful the views are through their French windows. We'll say thank-you for having me and I'll head off, back in my car as Avril gets on with her day, in the garden with the gooseberry bush, thinking happy thoughts about Esmé and Jenna while I'm in my car driving down the motorway listening to compilation tapes made for me when the people overtaking me in their faster cars hadn't even been born.

In November last year I did three village hall shows in three nights in Devon. Three John Baileys. Three Avrils. Three men in purple trouser saying they didn't think they'd like it but actually they thought it was quite good. Three types of homemade jam, three graduation photographs on the walls. Dara O'Brien stayed here, Dara O'Brien stayed here, Dara O'Brien stayed here. Driving back to Norwich after the last of the shows, the engine warning light came on, on the dashboard. As soon as I got back home to Norwich I decided that in the morning, I should phone Georgina.

The reason my car had been scrapped previously was because I'd ignored all those warnings. People who have kept their old tapes from the nineties all ignore warning signs on our dashboards. Georgina had said that her girlfriend was a mechanic, and that I could get in touch if I needed anything.

Georgina was delighted that I'd called and she gave me the name of her girlfriend's garage and said I should go there and she'd sort it out for me. She asked how I was getting on with Jamiroquai tapes she'd given me and I said ... *slowly*.

In the waiting room at Georgina's girlfriend's garage there are thank-you cards on the front desk and on the windowsills.

Who sends a thank-you card to their mechanic? What a nice thing to do.

Georgina's girlfriend told me she had a new apprentice, who was starting that day. She's seventeen and lives in their block of flats and she was talking to them one night, when they were having a cigarette by the back door. She told them she was obsessed with cars and that she hated sixth form. Georgina's girlfriend said well if you want you can come and work for me. They went up two flights to talk to her mum, who was delighted. What a sensible idea, she thought, and already on her first day she has decided 'this is what I want to do for the rest of my life. I want to work with cars.'

There were three of us in the waiting room at Georgina's girlfriend's garage. Three sad men waiting for our old cars to be mended. We all look like we need our MOTs. The lifeguard has told us we're not allowed to swim in the fast lane anymore. We're all impressed by Jurgen Klopp and were excited when Idles were quite good on Jools Holland. We didn't think that kind of thing happened anymore.

Georgina's girlfriend came over to say hi and she told me about the Polo. Georgina had bought it when she was seventeen, when they had just started going out with each other and even then it felt like an old car. They grew up in a village just outside Great Yarmouth and they weren't allowed to go anywhere or do anything. They were stuck. They hated it. Georgina passed her driving test and bought the Polo using money she'd saved up from her paper round and suddenly they weren't confined to Great Yarmouth anymore, they could go anywhere. They were constantly driving places, listening to Jamiroquoi and compilation tapes they had made for each other. They went to raves at Thetford Forest and that first summer with their car they went to every seaside town on the beautiful Norfolk coast. If you wanted to go somewhere, Georgina would drive you. Their car was always full of people looking forward to things.

After a while, Georgina's girlfriend came through and told me the car was all sorted. She said you don't need to pay, she was really happy she'd been able to play around with the old Polo again. I drove away. Happy that my car was okay.

For the next couple of years, I drove around in that Polo, listening to my old tapes, working as a support worker and occasionally driving across the country to do a show at a village hall.

One weekend I went back to the town I grew up in because my friend was getting married. The night before the ceremony we all went to the pub; real ale and crisps, telling stories, a big table and catching up with each other. It was fun, sitting in the pub with all my old friends from school.

The girl I used to walk to school with is a yoga teacher now. She lost her job at HSBC during the credit crunch, which now seems almost impossibly nostalgic. She took up yoga and that's what she does now. She teaches it for a living. Sitting in the pub the night before the wedding we played this game where she would ask us questions and we had to answer them without allowing ourselves any time to think. The question she asked me was 'what is the thing in life you are proudest of?'

The answer I gave was something I didn't realise until I heard it coming out of my mouth. My life is so different now.

She pointed at another of our friends, who'd been quiet all night, and said what is the thing you are afraid of? He started to get a bit emotional, and admitted to us all that he was in a bit of a mess. He had quite serious money problems and his car had just failed its MOT and he wasn't going to be able to repair it. He said he didn't know what he was going to do.

I'd just done four rural touring shows in a row in Cumbria and as four men with worryingly purple faces told me 'This is a long way to come, all the way from Norwich.'

I was so bored of driving. I really felt I needed a change. Life had been sliding for too long. I'd listened to all of those tapes. Sitting in that car I realised I was just becoming a different person. You can't lock yourself away with your memories. So I said if he wanted to he could use my car for a few months. I wasn't going to be needing it.

At work, we'd been told that the woman we supported had found a new place to live. It's much quieter there, a little bungalow, she'll be much happier there. This felt like a good time to leave. I told my boss I'd be taking some time off. He said he'd keep the job open for me. They always need support workers. Maybe I'll go back one day. It's hard to know what's going to happen next.

When I gave my friend the car I said this is the funny way the petrol cap opens and there are no electric windows, you have to wind them down, but don't worry that's good exercise for your elbows and there is no CD player and the radio doesn't work ... but the glove compartment is full of tapes. So now every time he drives to work, across the Humber Bridge, he drives while listening to those tapes that I made when I was a teenager. Sometimes he texts me to say what he's been listening to, or to ask about a song. Those tapes were such a big part of my teenage life. It feels like he is driving around in my scrapbook.

I really needed to listen to those tapes but now that I've heard them, I don't feel like I need them anymore. I'm glad I kept them for all those years though.

At work, someone dropped their favourite mug on the floor and it smashed, and they sobbed and I worry none of us are actually prepared for anything.

For two months last year I was happier than I've ever been before so I know I am still capable of it.

I guess at some stage Avril realised she was the kind of person who made jam from the gooseberries in her garden and helped out at the village hall.

I bet Natalie Imbruglia is so bored of singing *Torn*.

I decided to tell Georgina and her girlfriend what had happened to their car; the Polo that plays tapes. I said I wanted to let you know how much I loved that Polo. I gave them a thank-you card to add to their collection. I said that because you let me have that Polo I was able to keep on doing the job I loved for just a little bit longer.

It meant I'd been reunited with all of those cassette tapes. I said I know this might sound silly … but to show you how much I loved that car … I've written it a story.

# Acknowledgements

Thanks to Verity, Tom, Brian and all the staff at Summerhall. Special thanks to Katie Pope, Ross Sutherland, and Yanny Mac.

LAY OUT YOUR UNREST